M000029331

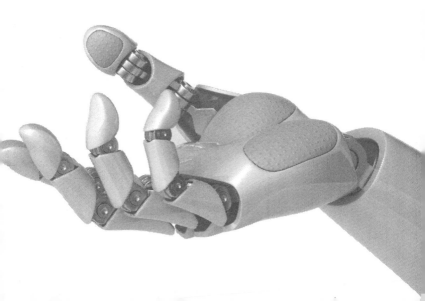

PIT STOP

Rebecca A. Demarest

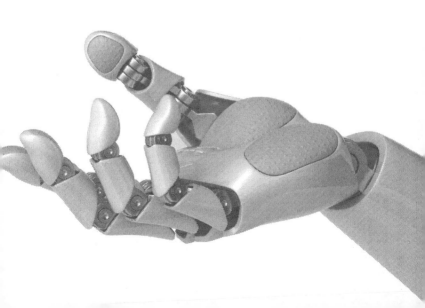

Published by WRITERLY BLISS

http://rebeccademarest.com

Book design by Rebecca A. Demarest

◦ ▬ ▬ ◦   ◦ ◦   ▬   ◦ ◦ ◦   ▬   ▬ ▬ ▬   ◦ ▬ ▬ ◦

The mass of tangled wires on Maevis's workbench twitched as she yanked a capacitor out. "Oh hush, you'll be right as rain in a moment." She had just picked up the soldering gun and wire to put in the new part when the alert on her long-range communicator pinged. Touching the activator patch on her right shoulder, she smiled and answered. "You've got Mama Maevis, refueling station Airco. Who's the rascal on my frequency today?"

"Mayday, mayday, God, is that even right, do you say that on a spaceship?" The link was tinny and breaking up, but Maevis could hear the panic in the male voice on the other end of the connection.

She dropped her tools and launched her chair across the room to the company computer array, earning a displeased yap from the Jack Russell terrier that had been sleeping in the middle of the floor. "Good enough, partner. What's your location and status?" She typed in a few commands to access the map of who was in the area.

"I...I don't know where I am exactly. Janice was navigating, and she's...she's hurt pretty bad. I stopped the bleeding, but she won't wake up. God, I'm a dead man."

Whoever was on the line, he wasn't one of their long-distance haulers; they didn't hire people as shakeable as this. "What's your name, son?"

"Tim. Timothy. Please, can you help me?"

"Okay, Tim, take a look at the board in front of you, you should see a line of numbers somewhere on the console. Do you see them?"

"No, I, yes, yes, there they are." He read them off to Maevis and she charted them into the system. He was not on any of the approved flight paths, but was pretty close to her refueling station, less than a day by thrusters.

"Very good, Tim. Now, can you tell me what happened? Do you have atmospherics, control?"

"I'm not sure. The alarms stopped sounding right before I figured out how to make this stupid radio work. I've never even been in a spaceship before this, Janice was the one..."

"Alright, I gotcha. Just listen to Mama Maevis. We'll get you down safe. I'm going to give you a list of things to try, do you think you can do that for me?"

He agreed readily and Maevis closed her eyes, envisioning a standard navigational panel. Running him through a checklist of specs, she determined he was in one of the high speed runners, designed to carry people fast and who didn't need to bring much with them. It wasn't a company standard, but she thought she could talk him through resetting the auto-pilot. After a half hour of instructions, she had the ship locked onto her beacon and coming in for a landing. As she hurried out to the refueling dock to prep the catch pad, Maevis conviced Tim to get his shipmate Janice down to the autodoc.

"Have you got the doc activated?" she asked him.

"What seems to be the emergency?"

Maevis grimaced at the memory the quasi-human voice woke in her, but she gritted her teeth, hauled the fueling cables over to the enormous anti-grav net, and started hooking them up.

"Her leg, it's just been...crushed."

It seemed morbid to be listening in on the kid's conversation with the machine, but Maevis didn't want to disconnect her link until she had them safely planetside. There was no telling if she'd be able to get the connection back.

"I see. I will do what I can." Maevis knew that line. That was the line the docs were programmed to respond with when the situation wasn't great. She remembered hearing the same thing right before the damn butcher had taken her right arm and a good chunk of her right ribcage. At least the technology had improved since then. Maybe this one would be able to save the girl.

The last fueling cable didn't want to engage, but with a flick of her carbon-steel fingers, it snapped into place. "Tim, I need you to go back to the control room for me."

"But Janice—"

"The doc is taking care of Janice. I need you to give me your coordinates again so I can get the net aimed." She didn't, really, but she did not want this boy watching Janice get her leg amputated and the standard cyber-interface installed. They didn't carry limbs shipboard, but every ship carried the interfaces because accidents happen, and the faster the interface was installed, the more likely the cybernetic prosthesis would work.

The boy read out his coordinates again and Maevis hurried back to her workstation to get the net up and running. Whatever ship these two were in was fast. A lot faster than anything in the company's fleet.

Maevis had just gotten the emergency net up and active when she heard the proximity alerts sound. It was a good thing she didn't have any company ships docked right now or she'd have had to clear them out for this. There was no telling what shape this kid's ship was in, or whether it would hold up to the impact of landing, or how much damage it would do to her little asteroid. She crossed her fingers and prayed silently to whatever gods would listen to get her through this one alive.

"Tim, buckle yourself in, I don't know how rough your landing is going to be. I'm going to lose our connection here as you enter the approach path because of the net, but I'll be waiting for you on the dock. I'll have a lei in one hand and a mimosa in the other."

"Sounds good, see you..." His voice crackled out and Maevis hurried to the window and raised the bamboo shades to watch as his ship streaked across the sky and fell straight towards the net. The terrier that had been asleep on the floor leapt to the bench at the window to watch with her.

"Better take cover, Angus," Maevis whispered, but the dog ignored her as usual. The two of them watched the ship tumble until it hit the anti-grav net and slowed, just enough that when it finally hit the water, it was hardly more than a love tap.

Maevis decided to leave the field on until she could determine how badly the ship was damaged and hurried down to the docks, though not before snagging her long-sleeved shirt and gloves from the hook by the door. The haulers joked that she was trying to protect her pretty skin from the harsh sun of her pit stop, and she never bothered to correct their misconception.

She struggled into the extra clothes as she skidded down the trail to the docks, and hit the boards just as the hatch popped on the ship and a young man in his late twenties tumbled out. She steadied him, gave him a once over, and took his chin in her hand to study his face for any signs of trauma. Satisfied he was in one piece, she leaped through the entryway and ran straight to the control room to ensure that the ship wasn't getting ready to blow and take them with it. Getting to know Tim better would just have to wait.

"So, Tim, can you tell me what happened?" Maevis studied panel after panel, but couldn't see anything amiss in the sensors.

"We were going along just fine...Janice had it all under control when we had an alert about something in the engine room and she went to check it out. All of a sudden I heard this really loud bang and ran back to check and found her pinned under a giant canister."

"Show me."

She could tell by the way he moved through the tight corridors that he was used to the big open hallways of one of the central planets: he huddled and shied from the bulkheads, unsure where they actually were in relation to his body. Maevis stood tall; they hadn't made a corridor yet that could challenge her five-foot-two height.

The engine room was a mess; she couldn't believe that there hadn't been any alarms or alert lights on in the cockpit with the amount of chaos she was seeing. But as she looked more closely at the primary drive mechanisms, it became clear that what she was seeing was mostly spare parts that should have been stored around the room. The drive itself was still contentedly humming away in standby. As a precaution, Maevis shut it down completely before heading down to the autodoc's bay.

While they walked, Tim kept up a stream of commentary of theories that Maevis mostly ignored, since he obviously couldn't explain what had happened any better than she could figure out. She'd spent years tending these ships on long-haul supply missions before her accident and they weren't much different now. But for the life of her, she couldn't tell what had happened in that room. There was no sign of a failure on the part of the engine—it was fully intact, but the room had definitely suffered some sort of explosion.

When the two of them reached the bay, Janice was already lying sedated in one of the recovery bays, a blanket neatly covering her up. Even with the blanket, it was obvious that one of her legs was much shorter than it should have been. Tim went to the patient's side and took up one of her hands, anxiously stroking the young girl's hair. There was almost ten years difference between the two of them and Maevis couldn't help but wonder why the two of them had been on the ship together, alone, and she prayed the young girl was Tim's sister.

"Doc, how is she?" Maevis couldn't bring herself to lift the blanket and check for herself.

The screen on the autodoc flickered to life. "Successful amputation and implantation below the right knee. Small contusion on back of head, presumably suffered in a fall after being struck in the leg. Stable, no concussion, expect a full recovery."

Of what's left, Maevis mentally added. "Is it safe to take her off ship?"

"Off ship? Why do we need to get off the ship?" Tim looked panicked and tightened his grip on Janice's hand.

"She is stable and is secured for transport."

"Thanks, doc, I'll take good care of her. You, get the gurney up and running. We need to secure the ship and get landside 'cause I don't particularly feel like hanging around a ship that just had an unexplained explosion, do you?"

"Point taken. I'll get her up." He hesitated briefly as he reached to tuck his arm under where her shin should have been, but then swallowed and picked her up, ever so gently, and placed her on the hovering plank at his side.

Maevis led the way back out of the ship and onto the dock, helping Tim maneuver the unwieldy anti-grav gurney. After they were cleared, Maevis punched in the code for a high-level stasis field, just in case anything else on the ship felt like exploding. She'd rather not have to rebuild her refueling dock...again.

She gave a piercing whistle and waited as the trees along the shore thrashed before giving way before Bessie. It was a good thing Maevis had a hand on the gurney, because Tim shouted and just about knocked Janice into the water at the sight of the island's five-foot-tall robot arachnid caretaker.

"Yes, Mama Maevis?" Bessie's voice was much more natural than the autodoc's since Maevis had programmed it herself, modeled after old-world actress Marilyn Monroe.

"Bessie, love, can you go get guest rooms one and two all open and aired out? Make sure the good sheets are on the beds."

"Sure thing, Mama Maevis." The machine briefly scanned the gurney, then turned back to her maker. "You'll be needing your scanner and kit then?"

"Thanks, Bessie, you're a doll." Maevis started dragging the gurney up the dock and Bessie kept pace long enough to reply, "And you're a peach!" before clattering off up to the house.

"What the hell is that thing?" Tim had recovered himself well enough to steady Janice's head as they started the hike up from the beach to Maevis's home and the island's command center.

"Well, it was the island's repair drone when I got here. But it was just so depressed with the limiters on it, so I took off the AI dampeners and gave her the legs. She picked the voice herself though. Her name is Bessie." Maevis smiled, remembering the robot's first teetering steps and excited giggling.

"And she picked that name herself as well?"

"Oh, no, that's just a shortening of her designation, Build and Servicer, Series E."

Tim stopped as they reached the top of the trail, frowning. "Isn't it illegal to remove AI limiters?"

Maevis made a rude noise. "They're like intentionally brain-damaging a child. I won't stand for them. Besides, what kind of harm could Bessie do out here on the ass-end of the galaxy? She's more likely to commit suicide out of boredom by leaping into that forsaken ocean covering this asteroid than she is to try and take over humanity. Now, let's get your girl here inside and comfortable, shall we?"

Her reasoning didn't seem to comfort the young man, but that didn't bother Maevis. She'd been questioned by the company before regarding her decision, but they seemed more interested in watching the robot's development in this controlled environment than they were in fining her for her indiscretion.

Bessie had just finished prepping the guest rooms when they reached the house, and she graciously bowed them into the room nearest Maevis's own. "I'll just go run and get your kit, b-r-b!" she trilled, and off she went again.

"Here, on three..." Maevis held Janice's shoulders, making sure to support her head on her forearms, and the two of them gently placed the girl on the bed. Tim started to adjust the blanket to more fully cover her, but Maevis stopped him. "I've got to start by taking some measurements."

She steeled herself a moment before pulling back the blanket. The girl's whole left leg, from just below the knee, had been completely severed. "Well, the good news is, she can still work on a ship if she wants to." Maevis took the bag that Bessie brought in and pulled out her holo-scanner.

Tim paused in his anxious pacing in the doorway. "I'm sorry, what?"

"Less than ten percent'll be mech. If she wants to work shipboard, the company will let her. If she passes the tests, that is. And if she still wants to after this."

He laughed, harsh and hard. "If her father ever lets her out of his sight again. But I doubt he'd have let her fly for the company even if she hadn't pulled this stunt."

Maevis carefully didn't look up from her scanning. "So who's she to you then, if you're not her father?"

"Not what you're thinking, I promise you that." Tim slumped into the wicker chair at the window. "She's my student."

"Your student." The holo-scanner beeped and she flicked on the display to get the measurements for Janice's new leg.

"She is the daughter of Viceroy Collins of Theseus. I'm her tutor. And right now? Her hostage." He groaned and slumped forward, dropping his head into his hands. "I am so dead. Take her to see the shipyard, he said. Maybe it'll show her ships are big and dirty and not for little girls, he said."

Maevis pulled a carbon-steel rod from her bag and started marking lengths on it. "Considering you're all the way out here and she was piloting a ship, I take it that didn't go over so well?"

Tim snorted and ran his hands through his hair. "She talked them into giving her a ride on the new prototype courier vessel. Then, as I'm throwing up in the toilet like the terrible spaceman I am, she knocks the pilot out, barricades me in the bathroom, and doesn't let me out until she's already launched the poor sap in an escape pod with a note to her father informing him that she's running away."

"Wait, if you were just up for a trial run, did you guys get swept for hydrogen ticks before you left?"

"Hydrogen what?"

"Well, shit. That's why you had an explosion. You left Theseus without a tick sweep. Hold on a minute." Maevis let out two separate whistles and within moments both Bessie and Angus were in the doorway. "We've got a tick ship at dock. Angus, guard." The little dog ran off, barking until he was answered by several other canine voices. "Bessie, can you get the rest of the crew and sweep the island? Full spectrum."

"Yes, Mama Maevis, right away." Bessie took off at a trot and a few moments later was followed out the front door by an assortment of mechanical beasties.

"Were those...more Bessies?" The look on his face was begging for a "no" answer, and Maevis was tempted to say yes. She never understood why people found the poor machine so frightening. She was sweet when you got to know her.

"No, those were other bots I've got programmed up to help around this place. I think the chef, the landscaper, and the maid, so it looks like dinner is going to be my responsibility tonight. Hope you like omelettes, 'cause that's about all I'm rated to cook." Maevis went back to the task of measuring and cutting the carbon-steel rod in her lap. As soon as she had it trimmed down, she mounted it in the socket of the interface on Janice's leg. Using the holo-scanner for a quick measure, she confirmed it was the right length to form the skeleton of the girl's new leg, then took the rod off and gathered her tools. "Come on, let's let the poor girl sleep and I'll make us something to eat."

Tim didn't eat much of the omelette Maevis made, but she wasn't too offended. It seemed like the man had a lot on his plate, and her appetite probably would have deserted her too, if she was in his place. When it was clear he was going to fall asleep over the dining table, Maevis led him back to his room and ordered him to bed, offering her usual array of sleeping supplements. It was sometimes hard for the company men to fall asleep landside after being accustomed to sleeping in the reduced gravity of their ships, so she had quite the selection. But he refused, thanking her before closing the door. Maevis went back to tidy the kitchen, then headed to her workroom with her kit and worked late into the night on Janice's new leg. She only took one break to go out and check on the status of the tick hunt.

Stretching on the front porch, Maevis let out a sharp whistle and it didn't take long for Bessie to respond.

"We seem to be clear, Mama Maevis."

"Excellent. Could you please keep scanning tonight? I just want to be entirely sure. I'd hate to be the epicenter of an outbreak."

"Absolutely, Mama Maevis."

"Thanks, you're a peach."

"And you're the bee's knees."

Maevis chuckled as Bessie rustled off into the forest again; she was never sure what endearment the machine would dredge up from the movie archive next. Making her way down to the docks, Maevis shed her long-sleeved shirt, reveling in the feel of the tropical breeze on her bare arm and shoulder again.

"Angus, how's it going?" The Jack Russell terrier was surrounded by a pack of mutts on the docks, all of whom were sprawled across the boards, mostly asleep. Angus let out a grumble and lay his head down on his paws.

"Nothing? Well, I'm sorry. But that is good for us. I'm going to run a sanitization on the ship, then you guys can go in to clean up whatever's left, deal?"

Jumping to his feet, Angus let out a sharp bark, his tail going mad. Maevis went over to the stasis control panel and sent a diagnostic wave through the ship, followed by a sanitization wave. It should kill anything of a biological nature on board, but having dogs trained to sniff out parasitic creatures was always a good backup. As soon as the waves had dissipated from the stasis field, she lowered it and opened the hatch for the dogs. They flooded in, all barking and baying for the hunt, but they were only inside for about ten minutes before they started trickling out.

Angus was last and spat a charred hydrogen tick at her feet. It was apparently the one that had exploded during flight. If that was the only one, then they should be good. Maevis dropped the carcass in the dock's incinerator and started back up the path, calling for the pack to come get their dinner.

The wave of fur at her feet kept her concentrating on her footing on the way back up to the house, so she didn't notice Tim standing on the porch until she was already at the front steps.

"So, that's what you meant about percentages. What are you, eleven, twelve percent?"

Maevis paused, her breath catching in her throat. She fought the urge to run, and instead just put the long-sleeved shirt back on. "Almost thirteen. Three ribs as well as the arm."

"Wait, are you that Maevis? Maevis Stanton? From the Icarus?"

"Why they had to name a ship after that idiot...you'd expect the whole damn thing to explode. Well, it nearly lived up to its name."

"I can't believe it! You're a living legend—no one knows where you went. Well...I guess now I know." Tim followed her as she shoved past him and into the house. "You were one of the best test pilots in the 'verse. Why are you hiding all the way out here?"

Maevis went to the kitchen, poured kibble out for the pack, then turned back to Tim. She waved her arm in his face. "Thirteen percent."

"So what, you can't fly anymore. You're a legend. People would pay money just to have their picture taken next to you. You have inspired whole generations of pilots and mechanics. They made a movie about you."

"I know. I donate every one of their damn royalty checks to cybernetic rights." Maevis put the kibble back in the cabinet and slammed the door.

"But don't you want to help people, tell them your story? I mean, even Janice loves you, your story is why she wanted to be a pilot."

Maevis ripped off her overshirt again, brandishing her metal arm, making her fingers wiggle so he could see the pistons and wire tendons flex. "You want me to encourage young people to do this? To sacrifice their very bodies to a company who doesn't give a shit about them, to be banned from the only job they were born to do just because they have one percent too much metal in their body? You want me to teach flying? How can I do that when I'm never allowed to pilot another vessel in this 'verse because the company lawyers are concerned that my presence on said ship could start a riot? Because you meat people are too fucking scared that I have the advantage?"

Maevis brought her arm down on the granite countertop of the kitchen island, cracking it down its center. She knew she was crying now, but there wasn't anything she could do to stop it. She used her meat hand to wipe the tears away, angry at herself for getting carried away. And on top of everything, she'd have to source a replacement for the counter now. She blamed it on the adrenaline rush from earlier in the day and lack of sleep now.

"I...I'm sorry." Tim was cowering in the corner of the kitchen, as far from her as he could get. He flinched as she stalked past him to the door. That only made her want to cry harder, hit him, anything to get that expression off his face, a look somewhere between pity and terror.

She stopped at the highboy beside the door and grabbed the whiskey bottle and a tumbler before turning back to Tim. "And if you tell that little girl in there who I am, or anyone for that matter, I swear to God, I'll hunt you down and I'll...I'll send Bessie to rip your arm off too." She slammed out of the kitchen and down the hall to her suite of rooms, not really caring if she woke Janice up, and proceeded to drain the whiskey bottle, a finger at a time, until the sun started to rise.

Tim found her the next morning in her workroom, the new leg assembly half completed. "Wow, you work fast."

Maevis frowned at the interruption. She had hoped to have a working intermediary limb done before either of her guests were awake. There was a small part of her, though, that relaxed at his casual greeting; she had not been sure how he would take her outburst the night before. She was never proud of losing her temper and she could never actually bring herself to hurt someone, but this was also not the first time she'd had to replace property she'd damaged in the course of said rage. If she cared to be honest with herself, she was never actually mad at the people or things she railed at. But it was hard to hit an incorporated entity that presented itself as a faceless mask of paperwork and automated call responses.

"I've had practice. Besides, all this leg needs to do is walk. The hardest part is getting the measurements right, and then stringing the wires in the right spots. But it's only two hinges, nothing realistic or lifelike. That'll have to wait until you guys reach the core planets again. I've got no exo-skins here." Maevis carefully soldered the connection she was holding before pushing back from her desk.

When she didn't yell at him, Tim moved into the room and sat in a chair by the door. Angus got up and trotted over, giving Tim a good sniffing over before accepting ear-scratches. "I was wondering why you use the long-sleeved shirts instead of an exo-skin. Don't you get hot in this tropical weather?"

Maevis made another connection before answering. "Yeah, but so do my electronics. I've got my arm and empty chest area filled with a long-distance com-link setup. That way I can talk to incoming ships a goodly way out, regardless of where I am on the island when they call. Exo-skins make it overheat, cotton does not." She plucked at her long sleeves for emphasis.

"Makes sense." he paused for a moment. "Look, I'm sorry for prying last night, I was completely out of line."

"I have more to be sorry about than you do. I shouldn't lose my temper like that. At least all I broke this time was a countertop. That's easier to replace than some of the specialized mechanicals around here." Maevis tested out the range of motion in the ankle joint, made a small tweak to the pivot, and tried again.

"Mama Maevis, sorry to interrupt," Bessie stood in the open doorway and Tim about fell out of his chair, having not heard the large bot come up the hallway.

"Whatcha got, Bessie?"

"Janice is waking, I figured you two'd want to be there for that."

"Thank you." Maevis picked up the artificial leg and started for Janice's room, Bessie leading the way and Tim following her. "How'd the hunt go last night?"

"The island is clean, Mama Maevis. The one that exploded on the ship seems to have been the only critter the ship had."

"Well, that's comforting, at least. Bessie, could you get the bots to start cutting some trees and shaping planks so I can make a new butcher-block top for the counter in the kitchen? It's broken again."

If a bot could look reproving, Bessie would have. As it was, her breathy voice dripped with recrimination. "Again, Mama Maevis? You really should know better by now."

"I'm improving, promise! And the last time was over four months ago! And that shipper was cheating!"

With a humph of disbelief, Bessie scurried out the door to start sourcing hardwood trees.

Tim went over to a window to watch the bot go. "She's worse than my mother at guilt-tripping."

"You'd think she was my mother and creator instead of the other way around. Now, let's go see to our young pilot, shall we?"

"Uh, Maevis...do you think, I mean, could you be the one to tell her? I don't think I can...I'm just not made out for this sort of thing. I'm just a tutor."

Maevis rolled her eyes. "Boy, she was smart enough to hijack a ship, she's certainly smart enough to figure out she's missing a leg. Buck up and get in there, she needs a friendly face."

Tim took a moment to gather himself, then knocked and pushed open the door. Maevis followed him in, the prosthetic hidden behind her. Janice was already sitting up in bed, the blankets thrown back, and was examining her shortened leg, trying to see the end of it and the interface already grafted into her skin.

Tim hesitated before going to the seat at the window and perching there. He cleared his throat a couple times before saying, "Janice, do you remember what happened?"

The young girl gave him a scathing look. "Well, we had that engine warning light come on and when I went to look..." she made a noise reminiscent of an explosion. "I'm guessing that's when this happened." She went back to inspecting the implant. Her flexibility was impressive.

Tim frowned at Janice's cavalier attitude towards her injury. "Your leg was crushed under some falling debris, and the autodoc couldn't do anything about it. I'm so sorry."

"Sounds about right." Janice swung herself around to the edge of the bed and stood without help, but then tottered as her balance was off. Bracing herself against the wall, she bit her lip, shaking off tears, and cleared her throat. "Well damn if this doesn't suck, but at least it wasn't my head." Her laughter at her own grim humor was just a touch manic, but it was better than hysteria. "How's my ship?"

Maevis fought not to smile. This was her kind of girl.

She moved into the girl's line of sight. "Flyable. The explosion was a hydrogen tick. Here, try this, it might help." She pulled the basic leg out from behind her and helped the girl to sit back down so she could attach it to the interface. "Now, it should respond like your meat leg did. Try to flex the foot."

Janice obeyed and the leg wiggled in response. "Oh, this is so cool! You know who else has a prosthetic limb? Maevis Stanton, the best damn pilot we've ever had. Now I'm just like her!"

Tim grinned and looked at the floor, but Maevis steadfastly ignored him. "If she'd been the best, she'd still be in one piece. Like you would be, if you'd remembered to let the flight deck do a sweep on your ship before taking it out."

"Oh, they did. They must have just missed a tick." Maevis frowned at that, but didn't interrupt the girl. "And Maevis was too the best pilot. The explosion wasn't her fault, I've looked at the records for the ship, and there was a flaw in the new drive system they were attempting. They fixed it in the prototype I flew here. But if Maevis had been any less of an incredible pilot and mechanic, she and her whole crew would be dead. It was a stroke of genius to land the Icarus on that asteroid covered in dry ice and then open the venting ports to put out all the fires."

Maevis helped Janice back to her feet. "You mean lucky that the asteroid was there. It still cost her arm and her clearance."

"But it saved her crew and the ship. And the ten percent rule is total bullshit, anyone knows that. I would put her at the helm of my ship in a heartbeat." Janice wavered a bit, but then stood steady. She took a few uncertain steps forward, then jumped up and down. "Hey, this is a sweet leg, thanks! Did you build it? It must have taken you weeks—how long was I out?"

"Just a day. I made this last night."

Janice let out a low whistle of amazement as she examined herself in the mirror on the back of the door. "This is pretty damn good for a day's worth of work. You're a whiz, thanks!"

"It's just a temporary one. When you get back to the central planets, they can make you one that's lighter, prettier, and they'll have exo-skins as well. Hardly anyone will be able to tell you have a mech leg unless you tell them."

Janice frowned and turned to the older woman. "Now why on earth would I want that? This is cool." She lifted her leg and wiggled her new mech bits at Maevis. "Besides, I don't want to go back to the central planets. Theseus is boring and my father won't let me do anything. I've already got a ship, I might as well just keep going to the outer rim and have myself some adventures."

Tim made a strangled sound and Maevis jumped, having forgotten he was even there. "Uh, were you expecting me to be going on these adventures with you?"

The girl made a face and sat back down on her bed. "Well, I was until you showed just how shit a spaceman you are."

Maevis sat beside the girl. "Janice, how old are you?"

"Thirteen." She held herself a bit taller and crossed her arms, daring Maevis to challenge her.

"Isn't that a bit young to go off adventuring on your own? I mean, you only have a year left before you're old enough to go into the flight academy."

"Maevis Stanton was flying her first ship at ten!"

"Maevis Stanton was flying her daddy's courier in circles out of any planetary transit routes, with him at the secondary controls, until she was fourteen and admitted to the flight academy."

Janice scowled. "I can already fly, I made my father's pilot teach me. I don't need the academy."

"Where do you think Maevis learned to think on her feet like she did? To repair her ship and build her own arm like she did? Hmm?" Maevis leaned over just enough to bump shoulders with the girl. "The way Tim talks, it sounds like your daddy doesn't much like the idea of you flying, but can he stop you from going to the academy? Truly?"

Janice scowled. "Not if I can get Mother on my side. He always listens to her."

"There you go, then. You have a plan of attack. You'll be able to get into the academy and then, five years later, you'll get your own ship."

Janice threw herself back on the bed. "But that's so far away! I don't want to wait that long to be behind the controls, not when I know how to fly now."

"Think of it this way, then. If you had known more before taking this ship, you'd probably still have your leg. And you're flirting with about eight percent mech right now. What happens when you make another mistake? When you lose a hand, an arm? Or more of that leg? Not only are you flying a stolen ship, you're flying mech, and the moment you land somewhere, you're going to get arrested. The company considers it a danger not only to your ship, but to others. But if you go to the academy, you'll learn how not to make any more mistakes. And then no one will be able to keep you off your ship."

Janice thought about this for a moment, sitting up to study her metal replacement. "It's not like it affects my ability, you know."

"It doesn't affect Captain Stanton either, but the company doesn't care about that. It cares about liability, and cyborgs are a liability shipboard, where confined spaces and prejudiced idiots can make a bloody mess. I'm sure you learned about the Haymarket Riots in school."

"Stupid Bostonians. First it's tea they throw in their harbor, then it's terrorists, then cyborgs. Just because they're afraid of them. Us." Janice's breath hitched a little and Maevis could hear the tears threatening to break through her defiance. "I guess it's us now."

"Now you're starting to get it. But enough with the heavy stuff—do you think you can manage some breakfast?"

The dark scowl that had settled over Janice's face was replaced by a wide grin. "I could kill for some bacon right now, do you have bacon?"

"Fresh off a transport two days ago. Come on, let's get you to the kitchen."

They had an uneventful breakfast, but Maevis could tell that Janice was tiring rather quickly. For all that medicine had advanced since the days of wooden legs and leprosy, it still took the human body a long time to get over the trauma of losing a limb. Maevis tucked the girl back into bed, leaving the door open a crack so Angus could keep an eye on her. The dog had become quite fond of the new amputee, and Maevis suspected it was due to a bribe of bacon.

"So, what's next? I mean, do you think she'll go home now?" Tim had stayed in the kitchen, setting a new pot of coffee to brew. "I only ask because I sure as hell can't fly that contraption back myself."

Maevis took the mug he offered and shrugged her shoulders. "I think so. For a little bit at least. Do you think there's any way her father will let her go to the academy? Because if he says no, I highly doubt he'll ever see her again. She's a bit of a hellion."

"Kinda like you." Tim raised his mug in salute, taking the sting out of his words. "And I have no idea what her father will do. I'm just praying I survive the trip home and the confrontation with him. I'm her eighth tutor, you know."

Maevis choked on her coffee. "Eighth? What the hell happened to the rest?"

"Four quit after a month with her, two went to a sanitarium for a while, the other two?" He shrugged. "I haven't been able to find that out yet."

"Why on earth did you take the job?"

Tim grimaced. "I owed Viceroy Collins. He got my little brother into the academy even though my family were governmentalists."

"Ah, the folly of our ancestors." Maevis snorted. "Now we just get to vote with our dollars. Which new flavor of Mountain Dew do you prefer? Buy now! All the real policy, set by their team of lawyers and designed to make us spend more money."

"And they do it so well."

Their conversation was interrupted by a chirrup from Maevis's shoulder. She held up a finger to Tim and hit the comm activation patch. "You've got Mama Maevis. Something I can do you for?"

"This is Company Raider Dauntless of Theseus. You have a stolen ship at dock; prepare for our landing. Do not try to lift off, we have your station under weapons lock." The comm patch let out a squawk and went dead.

Tim had gone pale, and he carefully set down his coffee cup. "Well, that took them less time than I expected. Should we wake Janice back up?"

"Let's go see how far out they are. No sense in waking her up to tell her bad news until we absolutely have to." Maevis led the way back to her monitoring station.

"They're about an hour out, it looks like." She leaned out the window and called Bessie in. The large bot was at the window within a minute. "Darling, we've got nosy company calling. Can you get the other bots and start preparations?"

"Sure thing, Mama Maevis." And Bessie was gone, followed by the rustling of smaller bots behind her.

"Preparations?"

"Surely you've noticed I'm not playing by all the company laws out here. Bessie and her kin need to be protected from narrow-minded company men who can't see beyond their regulations. They'll take cover in a system of maintenance caves under the island until I signal them an all-clear."

Tim nodded. "Good thinking. Anything I can do to help?"

"Just keep your trap shut about my babies." Maevis was busy at her panel, shutting certain access hatches so there was no way the company men could accidentally find their way into areas where she didn't want them. "But they're probably just here for Janice and the ship, and they'll be happy to leave once they have them."

"Hopefully me, too."

"And yes, you too."

It wasn't long before the ship's contrail glowed in the upper atmosphere of Airco, and Maevis made sure her arm was fully covered before leading Tim down to the docks to greet the incoming company ship.

The Dauntless made a textbook touchdown, and within moments the hatch opened and disgorged a regiment of security officers followed by the ship's captain. They secured the dock in quick fashion, one of the officers releasing the stasis field on the prototype ship before leading a few men on board.

The captain did not look happy at having wood and water beneath his feet instead of steel. "Which one of you is this way station's caretaker, Captain Stanton?"

Maevis stepped forward, offering a slight bow before responding. "That'd be me. Maevis, at your service."

"Since this station is not listed as having additional personnel, I assume you are Timothy Kennedy." The captain made a gesture to the armed man at his shoulder. "You are hereby detained for the kidnapping of Janice Collins and the theft of this prototype courier."

"What?" The officer had Tim's hands bound behind him before Maevis had a moment to even move.

"Tell us what you've done with Janice and we'll consider waiving the corporeal disenfranchisement."

"No, I..."

Maevis put herself between Tim and the captain threatening beheading. "Just a minute there, you've got the situation all fuddled up. Tim there didn't kidnap anyone. You see, there was a hydrogen tick in the prototype and it exploded, and Janice was hurt, but she's resting now up at the house..."

"My daughter was hurt?" The hard male voice that interrupted her came from the hatchway into the ship. Viceroy Collins ducked out into the sun and hurried down the gangplank.

"Sir, let me handle this..."

"Shut it, Chuck. What happened to my daughter?"

"Viceroy." Maevis gave a full bow to the man who was in charge of a whole planet's franchise. "I'm afraid she lost a goodly portion of her lower left leg. Sir."

The man paled, but otherwise showed no outward signs of emotion. "Take me to her, immediately."

Maevis led a whole parade of people back up from the beach: the viceroy, Captain Chuck, a string of security officers, and Tim trailing at the very end, his hands still bound. When they got to the house, they found Janice standing on the front steps, her hands on her hips and her new leg glinting in the sunlight.

"I don't care what you say, you were wrong to tell me I couldn't learn to fly. I did a damn good job flying that courier out here, before it blew up, but that wasn't my fault. You should let me go to the academy—"

The rest of her words were drowned out as her father swept her up into a massive hug. "I'm so sorry, princess. But don't you see now how dangerous flying can be?"

In an instant, Janice went from relaxed in her father's hold to rigid. "It wasn't the flying that was dangerous. It was a damn hydrogen tick that somehow managed to escape the scans."

Maevis watched with interest as the viceroy flinched at that last remark and reluctantly let go of his daughter. "Sir, might I suggest moving this conversation inside? It gets rather warm here during the day and I have a nice, private sitting room you two might talk in."

"Yes, thank you. Chuck, release my daughter's tutor, it appears he's not at fault in this after all." The rigid security officer saluted and did as he was ordered. Maevis ushered the crowd indoors, directing the security personnel to the kitchen and the viceroy and his daughter down the hall to the four seasons room. Viceroy Collins promptly shut the door and activated a cone of silence, the tell-tale shimmer glinting in the dark of the hallway. Maevis sighed and cancelled the text to her gardener bot about eavesdropping.

She got the security boys set up with snacks and drinks, and left them to kibitz with Tim about the horrors of riding herd on the walking catastrophe named Janice. It sounded like the girl was too intelligent for her own good and refused to acknowledge the ridiculous restrictions placed on her by her father. Good for her. Sucked for the people tasked with keeping her within said restrictions, but Maevis was proud of the little valkyrie. If she didn't watch herself, Janice really would become the next Maevis Stanton.

Maevis rubbed her metal arm through her sleeve; a little too like me, she thought. Who was there to keep kids like Janice from really hurting themselves? From ignoring not just the boundaries placed on them by society and their families, but the laws of physics and pure stupidity? There weren't many people of a level with Maevis's piloting skills, nor her electrical jury-rigging. And here she was at the shit-end of nowhere playing God on her own private island.

The door opened at the end of the hall. The excited tone of Janice's voice informed all of them that her father had caved on the subject of the flight academy, under condition that she adhere to even stricter rules in the meantime, including no more ditching her security detail. She blew a raspberry at her father, but the men in the kitchen silently toasted the proclamation. Maevis wondered which of them had been on duty this time when Janice slipped their watch.

The father and daughter duo came into the kitchen, Janice still a bit unsteady on her new leg, but managing to walk backwards as she spouted a steady monologue about her trip out, regaling her father with a report on how well the prototype ship flew.

The viceroy turned to his captain. "Chuck, we'll be leaving here as soon as we're refueled. Leave a detail behind to get the prototype into flyable condition and bring it back to Theseus, will you?"

The captain agreed, and started giving out orders to his men while Maevis chewed on her lower lip, trying to come to a decision. After Janice ran out to follow Tim and the men bound for the Dauntless, she signaled to the viceroy that she'd like a word. She waited until they heard the front door slam before settling onto one of the stools at the kitchen island, but the viceroy preempted her.

"That's a fine job you did on her leg in such a short time, Captain Stanton."

"Thank you sir, I have had a lot of practice." She took off her gloves to let her human hand breathe a bit. It was no use hiding her metal parts from this man, he knew all about them already. "I take it you didn't tell her who I was?"

"And have to listen about that for the whole ride back as well? No, thank you, I would prefer to spacewalk home." He sighed. "She thinks I'm just a mean old man, you know. But she's my only child. My wife, she can't..." He stopped and shook his head. "You never had children, I'm sure you can't understand."

Maevis drummed her fingers on the countertop, and then took the leap. "That's where you're wrong, sir. I know what it's like to love a creature as if it's your own child. My dogs here, my machines, I wouldn't know what I would do without them, sir, which is why I can't understand why you planted a hydrogen tick on her ship. Sir." she added for good measure. Her human hand was shaking, but she splayed it on the counter so the viceroy wouldn't see and stared him in the eye until he had the grace to look away.

"It wasn't supposed to happen like this. The pilot who took her up was supposed to just use it to scare her. A small controlled explosion on an underfed tick is virtually harmless. And then she had to go and pirate the whole damn ship." The viceroy sat down hard in one of the chairs at the table. "What kind of thirteen-year-old girl can take over a security prototype ship?" He dropped his head in his hands.

"Yours, sir. Your incredibly intelligent, independent, and willful child. And she's not done making changes in this world, mark my words." Maevis came across the room to sit beside the viceroy and only hesitated a moment before putting her hand on his shoulder. "And you just want to protect her, I get that. And...I think I can help you there."

The viceroy looked at her over his hands. "How? I can't even control her."

"Not control her, but...look. You agreed to let her go to the academy, right?" She was sure he'd only done it out of guilt for what his actions had wrought, but he nodded and she continued. "Why don't you put in a transfer order for me? Get me off this rock and back to the main system, in a teaching post at the academy." He started to say something, but she held up her hand. "I've got a couple conditions, though. I don't want a classroom position. I want to be shipboard. None of this nonsense about ten percent. I am a damn good pilot and I can't teach these young idiots anything from a desk."

She watched him think about it for a moment, weighing the guidelines against having the Maevis Stanton watching over his daughter at the Academy, and then weighing that information against the fact that she knew about the hydrogen tick and just how damaging that kind of information could be in the hands of someone who was pissed off at him.

He nodded, short and sharp. "I think we can manage that. You said a couple of conditions though. What's the other?"

Maevis grinned. "Tell me, Viceroy, are you a fan of Marilyn Monroe?"

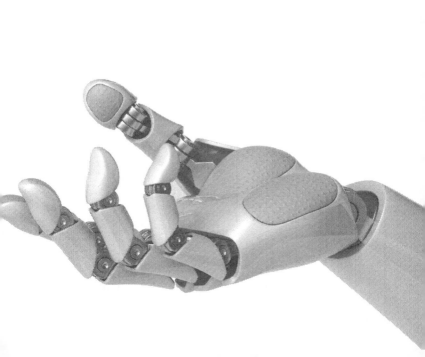

This book is laid out using
Athelas by José Scaglione and Veronika Burian from TypeTogether
and LIBRARY 3AM by Igor Kosinsky from Bēhance.
Cover image sourced from Shutterstock and created by koya970
Printed in the USA by KDP and Amazon.

Made in the
USA
Lexington, KY